WELCOME TO TRINITY

WELCOME TO TRINITY

Entanglement Book 0

Phil Oddy

CHAPTER 1

The first time that Authority Oficier Simeon Lagrange came to Clar's flat, they didn't let him in.

Even from outside he loomed, his face filling the DoorCom screen. It was a one-way link, but Clar couldn't help feel trapped by his stare. They were glad they didn't have the holo version. They did not need him manifesting in their hallway.

'Clar Triebel?' he asked, stepping back from the camera and holding up an Authority identity token so that Clar could see it.

'Yes,' mumbled Clar.

Their instinct was to deny it. They'd been using other names, but this man, Lagrange, obviously knew who they really were. It seemed pointless to pretend to be someone else.

'Clar Triebel, Rosaan12?' he doubled-checked. 'Only the name that Administration has registered for this dwelling is a Mr Barginssen and... I need to talk to Clar Triebel, and only them.'

OK, so this Lagrange absolutely knew who they were. The reference to Clar's broadcast channel was pointed. They doubted that there were any other Clar Triebels in Trinity,

Triebel being a quintessentially Rosaanan name, but this guy absolutely had the right one.

The right one for what?

'Can I come in?'

'No,' said Clar.

They didn't know if they were allowed to refuse. They didn't know if that was an actual question, or a polite prelude to violence.

"We asked nicely. Now we're going to blow your house down."

'OK.' Lagrange lowered the token and stepped forward so that his face filled the screen again. He dropped his voice. 'Only it's going to be tricky to have the conversation I'd like to have with you while I'm standing in the street.'

'Do we have to have it?' asked Clar.

They didn't think there was any conversation that they wanted to have with an Authority Oficier. They had contacts in Authority - cadets mostly, but a few Junior Oficiers as well. Those contacts had left them with the distinct impression that it would be dangerous to venture any further up the chain of command.

'We don't. But I hoped you would feel you could trust me.'

Clar thought it should have been obvious from their actions thus far that they didn't. They weren't sure what Lagrange had done to show his trustworthiness, either. They weren't just going to take his word for it.

They said nothing else, there didn't seem to be a need. They just hoped that the Oficier at the door would take the hint.

Lagrange took in a deep breath and sighed noisily.

'I liked your piece about the election.'

Clar couldn't help but react to that. They let out a loud, spluttered exclamation.

'Election! That's not what we'd call it in Rosaan. And it's not like my homeland is a paragon of democratic principles.'

'Quite,' agreed Lagrange. 'We have issues. But you really got under the skin of the thing. Anyone can see the problems with the poll - who runs it, where it happens... But the campaign finance bit? Implicating Ort'a?'

'Strictly speaking, I don't think I suggested that Ort'a had done anything wrong. I don't know that he knew where his funding was coming from.' Clar corrected him.

Lagrange whistled.

'True, true...' He paused. 'But we all know that he should have done, right? And that even if he didn't, someone in Opposition did?'

'There's a difference between what I know and what I can broadcast,' Clar observed.

They hadn't meant to get involved in this conversation, hadn't meant to have a conversation at all. Lagrange spotted this.

'You see, this is nice!' He took a step back and looked around. 'But if you're not going to let me in, then I might have to take off. Not a good look, for me, this. Talking to a brick in a wall.'

Clar said nothing. Despite themselves, they were warming to Oficier Lagrange. They wondered what he wanted. Not enough to let him in. But...

'I'm leaving you something,' said Lagrange. 'I think it will be helpful. You're wading into some dangerous waters and I'd hate for the sharks to smell you coming.'

He bent down, disappearing offscreen for a moment, before his face reappeared as he straightened up.

'I've locked it to your voice print. So it's no use to anyone else. But that won't be immediately apparent, so I'd come and pick it up before someone swipes it off your doorstep. Have a nice day, Clar Triebel.'

And with that, he disappeared from view.

Clar stood, staring at the blank screen for a few deep breaths, while they calmed their racing heart. That was a strange conversation. On the other side of it, they were surprised at how they felt. Not frightened, but exhilarated, excited. They wondered what the Authority man had left for them.

They went to the window, in time to see Lagrange disappear down a side street. It was quiet, mid-shift, pre-lunch, so he was easy to spot. Not everyone worked in the factories, though. If they wanted to pick up their gift, they shouldn't hang around.

Clar grabbed their Com and left the apartment, scampering down the stairs and through the shared hallway. Most of Clar's neighbours were out at work, but they didn't want to risk bumping into someone unexpectedly. They weren't, after all, Mr Barginssen.

The heavy front door swung open, only just clearing the small box that was sitting on the step. Clar bent over and picked it up. The box was plain, but the dimensions and weight were familiar. They instantly knew what it was.

They ran back up the stairs and used their Com to buzz themselves back into the flat. The trusty but ancient ComE device that had seen them all the way from Rosaan to the edge of Trinity and served them well for the first year inside the walls…

Inside the box was a new model. A brand new model, in fact. A pristine ComM, although without its original packaging. There was also a note.

GLAD YOU DECIDED TO ACCEPT MY GIFT, it said, in scrawled capital letters. Clear and efficient, but also sloppy and rushed. *A measure of the gifter?* I'VE MADE SOME MODIFICATIONS. NOTHING SHADY, BUT THIS SHOULD BE MORE SECURE THAN THE MODEL YOU'RE USING.

Clar didn't like this. It felt intrusive. They needed some time to think.

Regardless, an offer had been made. They had to decide if they wanted to take it. That was tricky, because they didn't know what it was going to cost them.

Their independence, at a minimum. Maybe that wasn't so bad. They'd been on their own for a long time.

Their integrity? Would it be possible to work with Trinity Authority without being compromised? Maybe so, if this Lagrange was the outlier that they sensed he might be. But they needed to be sure.

They opened the refrigerator door and put the new Com device inside before closing it.

Time. Give it some time.

Time to think.

As the call connected, Clar checked their escape routes again. They were standing outside, in the middle of the square, a clear view across the grass in all directions. There were plenty of side streets, and main roads leading from the corners, all a quick dash from where they stood.

Mid morning traffic was at a minimum, only a half dozen pedestrians going about their business. If they had to make a run for it, then there was nothing more hazardous than a low wall to hurdle. This was as good as it was going to get.

They'd given it time. They'd been able to think. They'd made their decision. They were too intrigued to leave it alone.

'Lagrange,' said the voice on the other end.

Clar kept the call to voice only. Their new Com could hologram, of course it could, but this conversation needed to be low key. It was bad enough that they were having it outside, but they also needed to be safe.

Maybe this was a mistake.

'It's me,' said Clar.

It had been a week since the Authority agent had left the Com for Clar. A week in which the device had mostly stayed in the fridge. They'd taken it out one time, for a trip down to the docks so that Fricker could give it a once over.

'So, you found my contact details.'

They'd been pre-programmed into the Com. It was clear what its intended use was. What Clar didn't understand was what he wanted from them.

'You gave me an Authority device,' they said, sternly. 'Who's listening?'

Again, they checked the exit points, checked out the pedestrians, calculated the angle they'd have to move at to avoid the tram now clattering along one side of the plaza. There were no signs of hidden Authority personnel that they could see.

Of course, it was the ones that you couldn't see that you needed to be ready for.

'I gave you a *secure* device,' replied Lagrange. 'No one is listening. Except me.'

'And I have to take that on trust?'

They would not take it on trust.

'No, listen to your tech guy,' said Lagrange. 'Didn't you take it to Fricker?'

Clar was thrown. That he knew about Fricker wasn't a surprise. Fricker's services were legendary. But he'd wanted them to take the device to Fricker. He must have known what Fricker would say.

'Fricker said he couldn't hack it. Couldn't promise that he knew what it could do,' Clar said.

'Fuck!' exclaimed Lagrange. 'That boy keeps his mouth shut too well.'

'What do you mean?'

Clar was feeling out of the loop.

'Fricker set the thing up. He took a standard ComM, removed all the traces, installed Authority security levels, then hacked the Authority security levels and locked the whole thing down. There isn't a more secure device in Trinity. No one can hear you whisper, let alone scream…'

'He said…'

'He takes his instructions too seriously,' muttered Lagrange. 'I told him that no one should know what he'd done for me. I assumed he understood that didn't include you.'

'Right.' Clar remained sceptical. 'None of this helps me. I still have to take your word for it.'

'You do. That's unfortunate. But maybe that's just the way it has to be. I know where you live, obviously, but no harm has come to you because of that knowledge. I know that you're not currently at home, even though you think I will assume that you are…'

Clar's heart leapt into their throat. That was exactly what they thought. The whole reason that they were standing in the middle of an open square in front of their flat was so they could see what was happening, if Lagrange was going to make a move when they made contact. It was about keeping options open and escape a possibility.

But he knew. How did he know?

Clar flicked their head back and forth, examining the immediate environment for clues, for suspicious activities. There were none.

'How did you know?'

'You have some serious trust issues, you know? But I think I know a bit about why…'

'How? Why? What do you have on me? Where are you getting your information from?'

'Hold on, hold on…'

Lagrange's was aiming for "soothing" with his tone, Clar could tell, but there was panic there, showing in the speed with which he uttered the syllables. That was strangely reassuring. It was like he was worried that Clar's paranoia was about to lead to them cutting the call, like that wasn't something he wanted to happen. And not just because it would spoil a complicated entrapment. Just because.

It sounded like he cared.

After all this time, all the people Clar had met - every friend, every nemesis, everyone who had helped them, everyone who had betrayed them - had made Clar a pretty good judge of character. They could read tone and inflection, and nuance and everything that wasn't being said.

It surprised them, but in Lagrange, they heard an ally.

'OK,' said Clar.

'OK?'

'OK. I believe you. Not sure I trust you, but it's early days. Whatever that it is you want me to do, I'm open to listening.'

'That's all I'm asking at this point,' said Lagrange. 'I'm very pleased to hear you say that.'

'Don't push it,' warned Clar. 'You're not the first person from Authority I've had dealings with. I have liked none of them.'

'None of them were me.'

Clar could hear him grin as he said it.

'Don't push it,' repeated Clar. 'I mean it.'

'Right, got you.' Lagrange dropped to a more serious register. 'I have a proposal I'd like you to consider. I think I might be best if I made said proposition in person.'

'Where? When?'

The call dropped. Clar stared at the Com screen. Lagrange had cut them off. Clar felt a firm hand on their shoulder and jerked around in shock.

'Sorry to startle you,' said Lagrange, fighting to suppress the return of that grin.

Clar took him in. They could see the fray of his collar, the dirt under his fingernails. There was a faint, lingering trace of alcohol on his mint-scrubbed breath.

He wasn't an impressive sight, up close. He was a human one, though.

'No time like the present, though?' asked Lagrange. 'Shall we take this inside?

CHAPTER 2

Clar watched a third miniTram pull up behind the other two. Now they were all waiting. Only the first was level with the platform, so no one could get on or off the rest. The front one had long since closed its doors in anticipation of the light in front of it turning green, so, now, no one could get on or off of that one either.

That conversation with Sim, almost four years ago, had been the start of it. Since then, he'd been a useful connection, a trusted mentor, and a loyal friend. Sim's beat was the activities of the Black Knights - the loose collective of gangsters, assassins and thieves who bled Trinity daily. Clar's journalistic focus was the activities of the corrupt and despotic mayor of Trinity, Stam Chaguartay, whose grip on power was only getting tighter.

Those two things shouldn't have overlapped. Not in the way they did. Not to the extent they did.

The light wasn't turning green. It hadn't done for twenty minutes. Nobody was going anywhere. From their first-floor window, Clar saw a familiar, shambolic figure shuffle across the square. He looked much the worse for wear, which wasn't unusual these days.

He was punctual, though, always on time. Clar appreciated that. Given the assorted levels of chaos between which Sim lived his life, they somewhat admired it, too.

Their work had become inextricably linked. The Black Knights were given carte blanche to exploit every inch of Trinity's sprawling underground by the tolerance they enjoyed from Chaguartay's regime. Chaguartay, in turn, had a private army of thugs, more than happy to rig elections, squash dissent and murder opponents for him. It had made sense for the two of them to join forces, share leads, scratch each other's backs.

Clar left the window and filled a jug with ice from the machine, then went to the tap and topped it up with water. They took a lemon from the bowl and quartered it. All four quarters went into the water before they placed the jug in the middle of the table.

Clar wrote the stories, which were largely ignored by most of Trinity's downtrodden citizens, but were picked up by enough of the chattering classes in Ashuana and Rosaan to fund their modest lifestyle. Sim solved the crimes. Whether he could arrest anyone for them was another matter. Usually he couldn't, but at least justice was theoretically possible, even if it wasn't actually done. They made a good team.

Is there beer in the fridge? Clar checked. There were two bottles behind the butter, lying down on the second top shelf. Clar removed them and hid them in a cereal packet, which went back into the cupboard it had come from.

The problem was that, lately, Clar had questioned why they were doing what they were doing. It wasn't what they'd expected; it wasn't why they'd trekked over the best part of a continent to get here.

They'd left Rosaan, rejected by the society that had raised

them, and struck out for somewhere new, somewhere exciting, somewhere they could be themselves. From a distance, Trinity had looked very different. Steeped in tradition that radiated from the Citadel in the centre, at the same time an industrial powerhouse with the white-hot fire of technological progress burning brightly.

Now they were here, they spent most of their time explaining how terrible it all was. It needed to be done. People deserved to have their stories told, but increasingly Clar wasn't certain that they had to be the person to do it.

The DoorCom beeped, and Clar let Sim through the front door. They heard the irregular thumping of him ascending the stairs. Carefully, then with confidence, then two at a time. The thud of a toe caught on the step, the yelp of shock and irritation, the fall back to the half landing had all been inevitable. It sounded painful.

Clar thought maybe it was time to leave Trinity. Not to go home, necessarily. But they probably needed to be somewhere else. Whatever they'd thought that they would find in this city, it wasn't here. Trinity wasn't a healthy place for anybody. Just looking at what it had done to Sim was enough to confirm that.

Clar went to the door of their flat and opened it manually, just in time to see Sim lurch to the top of the stairs and fall forward before any adverse momentum from his exaggerated swaying caused him to tumble back down.

'Rough night?' Clar asked, as they stepped aside to let him in.

'I haven't slept,' Sim mumbled through his hand as he rubbed his face.

This wasn't unusual. Sim rarely seemed to sleep.

'You should look after yourself,' Clar scolded.

'Like you look after yourself?'

Sim made it to the end of the hallway and into the kitchen,

where he threw himself into the nearest chair.

'I see you've got the jug out,' he sneered. 'Where have you hidden the beer?'

'You don't need beer.'

Sim looked doubtful about that. Clar poured some water into a chipped glass, then rotated it so that Sim was less likely to cut his lip open on it.

'What's new?' they asked.

This was always how the conversation opened. A briefing, the latest intelligence, some names, some Com details, the start of the next story. Clar had meant to lead by saying that they were thinking of leaving. Old habits died hard, though.

'Nothing's new.'

Sim coughed on the water, then pulled a face like it was poisoning him, but Clar caught the wince that betrayed the pain that flashed as the iced water washed past his uncared-for teeth.

Sim put the glass on the table.

'Same old shit,' he grumbled. 'Same old shit. Why do we do it?'

Drink seemed to do many things for Simeon Lagrange. If he was to be believed, it made him sharper, more instinctual, better at his job. Clar wasn't certain about any of those things, but it did make him more relaxed, more pleasant. Sober Sim wasn't someone they'd had a lot to do with - he wasn't a regular visitor, apart from anything - but they didn't particularly enjoy his company. It was one reason people tolerated the rest of his behaviour. You knew it could be so much worse.

Something it had never done for him before, though, was to make him philosophical. Sim was a man of action, a decisive man. Thinking was generally focused on solving puzzles, on deduction, even if the deduction regularly bypassed his brain and came straight from his heart, or his gut.

This was a new side of him. Clar was wary.

'I don't know that I can. Not any more. I think I need to leave.'

There, they'd said it.

'Leave? OK,' Sim seemed unbothered, which probably meant that he'd got the wrong end of the stick. 'Just tell me where you've hidden the beers and I'll be here when you get back.'

'Not leave the flat,' explained Clar, patiently. 'Leave the city. Leave Trinity.'

'For good?' Sim paused.

Clar waited for him to get worked up at them, but he didn't. He just held the silence until it got too uncomfortable for Clar not to fill it. It was a thing he did, a thing Clar knew he did. It didn't make it any easier to resist.

'Yes, for good.'

'You always say that,' objected Sim.

Clar had said it, before. Once, maybe twice. No more than that.

'No, I don't.'

'No,' agreed Sim. 'You don't. So why are you saying it now? People need you, Clar.'

'You, maybe. But you're not people, Sim. You're you. Also, you'll be fine.'

Sim rubbed his chin. He didn't seem so sure.

'We make a good team.'

'We did.'

He was right; they did. But Clar was no longer sure why that was important, what it was for.

'What about Jo Jo?' asked Sim.

That was a low blow. Jo Jo was Sim's son, and he and Clar had cultivated what they both described as "a thing". He had slept on Clar's sofa for a while, after a fallout with his mother. Clar wasn't aware of much discussion about him moving in with his dad. They had never seen Sim's place, but they could imagine, and they understood.

It hadn't been a problem. They enjoyed Jo Jo's company and eventually he'd graduated from the sofa to their bed. It wasn't any more than that, although Clar would admit that they were incredibly fond of the fresh faced idiot.

'He cares about you,' Sim suggested, poking at the weak spot he thought he'd found.

'Jo Jo will be fine.'

That was their last defensive word on the matter. Lagrange moved on.

'You shine a light, help people understand.'

'It's only words, though, Sim. And the people who really need to hear them aren't listening. I've got no audience in Trinity. It's all liberal intellectuals in Ashuana City and religious fundamentalists back home. And they're only listening because it makes them feel superior…'

Sim was about to tell them they did themselves a disservice, that one mind changed, however close to home, was one step closer to putting things right. And he wasn't wrong.

But he wasn't right, either. Trinity was broken. Maybe not doomed, but destined for a long, hard pull out of the depths it had allowed itself to be plunged into by its cruel, self indulgent, master.

'You want to make a difference?' Sim asked.

His voice was low, rumbling, an earthquake preparing to rip up the ground. Clar took a step back.

'You want to make a difference?'

He phrased it like a question, but Clar heard a demand. They would make a difference, had to make a difference.

'I want to make a difference.'

'You've not been answering your Com.'

The apparent non sequitur was something Clar had got used to. It would make sense in a moment.

'I had to get a new one,' they said. 'The previous one had a run in with a TransPod.'

'Shame,' said Sim. 'That was a nice bit of kit.'

He stood up, stretching out his back with a grimace. He really wasn't in good physical shape.

'I know,' admitted Clar. 'It held sentimental value, too.'

Sim scoffed, and crossed the kitchen floor to the full length cupboard, which he opened. He took out a box of breakfast cereal, inspected the front of the pack.

'These aren't good for you, you know? They're full of chemicals. That's how they're so purple.'

He opened the top and extracted a beer bottle. Clar's shoulders dropped. It hadn't taken him long. They suspected he'd known from the moment he'd stepped into the room.

Sim placed one bottle in his trouser pocket, which turned out to be efficiently deep. He held the other in his right hand.

'ComN?' he said.

The new model had been out for a matter of weeks. Clar nodded. It had cost them a small fortune.

'Get it fixed up,' said Sim, popping the top off the bottle on the worktop. It took a chip out of the trim. Another chip out of the trim. Sim was a regular visitor. 'You know where Fricker lives?'

Of course, Clar knew where to find Fricker. They nodded their agreement.

'Good. Get it sorted, call me.' Sim made for the door. 'You want to make a fucking difference? I've got someone for you to meet.'

I could just leave anyway, Clar thought as the door slammed closed at the end of the hallway. But they knew they wouldn't.

17

Fricker's workshop was little more than a shack, one in a row of them. At the front, it opened up onto the street, which is where Fricker sat when he was working.

That was because there wasn't any room for him inside the workshop, which was filled with boxes, and racking that held more boxes, of a density that increased as you went towards the back. Every box had wires emerging from it - from the top, out of tears in the side - like roots sprouting in all directions.

At the back, Clar could just about see, was a door. They thought it unlikely that it was ever used, given how inaccessible it appeared. Behind the shack was a warehouse, and that was probably where the door led.

Most of Docklands was warehousing. The shacks might, at one time, have been storage cupboards at the back of the warehouse, before an enterprising someone took the wall out and opened them up to the street.

Now they were workshops and corner shops and drug dens. They provided shelter and a floor that, even if it wasn't clean, was at least separated from the street by a gutter, which was the next best thing. From the blankets piled behind one rack, Clar assumed Fricker slept in his.

Fricker turned Clar's new ComN over in his hands, inspecting it with admiration through the goggles that he wore most of the time. Clar wasn't sure if they were necessary, if they helped correct a vision defect, or if he'd just forgotten he was wearing them.

'Shiny,' he said. 'Not seen many of these yet. It's the latest model.'

Clar was aware of this, of course. It was why they were now poor.

'Can you still fix it?' they asked.

'Is it broken?' Fricker grinned. 'They just don't make them

like they used to, do they?'

'You know what I mean,' said Clar. They knew he knew exactly what they meant. They didn't have time to play games. '*Fix* it. Like the other one.'

'Other one?' asked Fricker. 'I don't know what you mean. However, I do know what you're talking about, and the good news for you is… Yes, yes, I can.'

Clar breathed a sigh of relief.

'Amazing,' they said. 'I wasn't sure if it took time to figure these things out. I was worried it was too new.'

Fricker raised his goggles and stared at Clar, eyeball to eyeball.

'It does take time,' he said sternly. 'It takes a very long time. No one else can do this for you. You realise that, don't you?'

Clar got the impression that they were about to pay dearly for a second time, in order to make this new Com secure enough to use with confidence. Fricker was right, though. Sim wouldn't trust anyone else to do this work, so Clar wouldn't either.

'I do,' nodded Clar. 'Don't be under any illusions - I appreciate and am in awe of your genius.'

'That's very kind.' Fricker turned and rummaged in a box on a table behind him. 'But I have a significant advantage over every other hack in this city.'

'Really?' Clar was worried that this transaction was about to turn into a conversation.

If they were honest, they wanted to get the work done and get out of Docklands. They didn't exactly feel safe in this area, and with good reason. They knew they were already a target for harassment. They didn't want to attract any more attention than they needed to.

'Really,' said Fricker, finding what he was looking for and spinning around to give it to Clar.

It was a ComN device, the same as the one Clar had bought and Fricker now held in his other hand. It had the same configuration of buttons, the same dimension of screen. Every tweak that had been made to ensure that this model was incrementally more desirable than the one before was in place. Clar flipped it over. There was a large letter N etched into the metal casing.

It was definitely a ComN device. But whilst Clar's was new, and unmarked, free of chips or scratches, this one looked old. It appeared battered, with the grease and detritus from a thousand fingerprints stacked up in its grooves and edges.

It couldn't be, though.

'You've certainly put this one through its paces.' Clar handed it back. 'How did you get an advanced model?'

They were certain that Administration wasn't in the habit of sending early release Coms out to backstreet hacks.

'Not an advanced model.' Fricker raised an eyebrow mysteriously.

'Then how…?'

'I know a man from the future,' grinned Fricker, putting the battered Com device into his pocket. 'That's how I know.'

Clar narrowed their eyes, looked at him carefully. However ridiculous that statement appeared to be on the surface, he meant it. He believed it.

'That's handy,' they said, humouring him. 'Time travelling tech support.'

'Yeah,' said Fricker. 'That too.'

He scrutinised Clar's Com one more time. Apparently satisfied, he placed it carefully on the table behind him.

'I can do the work.' He turned back to Clar and fixed them with an intense stare. 'But he gave me a message, too. For you.'

'Who did? Sim?'

'Don't leave town. We need you.'

Clar returned the stare with incomprehension. What had Sim been saying about them? Why would he be telling Fricker to beg them to stay like this? And "we" - in what way did Fricker need them?

'I don't… what's Sim been saying? He's got this obsession about me serving the greater good, but to be honest…'

'I'm not talking about Sim.' Fricker cut them off without breaking the stare. 'The man from the future. He told me.'

A chill descended Clar's spine. This was getting too weird.

'He told you what?'

'He told me you needed to stay. Sim needs you. Then… afterwards…'

Fricker trailed off, looking down, releasing Clar from the intensity of his attention. He busied himself rearranging some miniature tools that were sitting on top of a stack of boxes.

'After what? What's going to happen? Is something going to happen to Sim? What do you know?'

The questions poured out of Clar. They couldn't help themselves. This was not their usual interview technique. This was an urgent need to know which gripped them tight inside and squeezed out demands for information.

Fricker looked back at them, his gaze more distant this time.

'I can't tell you,' he said. 'I don't really know. That's what they said, word for word. That's what I had to tell you.'

'You said "we". "We need you". Who needs me?'

Fricker shrugged.

'I literally have nothing else to tell you. I don't know who he is.'

'So you don't know he was from the future? He could just be some crazy off the docks?'

Except he knew I planned to leave Trinity. That's a well informed crazy.

'He gave me the Com,' replied Fricker. 'That was enough

21

to convince me, but if your journalistic instinct says that's not sufficient, then...'

The silence between them threatened a slew of new questions, but Clar realised Fricker wouldn't be able to answer any of them.

'How long will it take?' they asked.

'Couple of hours, maybe less.' Fricker rubbed his nose. 'I guess it's going to be hard to let you know if I've got your Com...'

That was a good point. Clar needed the device back as soon as possible. They had things to do, people to meet. People Sim wanted them to meet.

'Can I wait?' they asked.

'Don't like to be watched,' grumbled Fricker. 'It'll take longer. Why don't you grab a drink? Eamer's is around the corner. I'll send a runner when I'm done.'

Clar knew about Eamer's, of course they did, but their aversion to Docklands had precluded them from ever having the chance to check it out. On the outside, it was exactly as uninviting as they'd assumed it would be. On the inside, it was much the same as any other place they'd found to drink in Trinity. Booths around the edges, tables in the middle and a long bar with plenty of booze behind it.

Clar knew about Eamer, of course, as well. The Black Knights didn't have a leader, they were more of a loose cooperative of like-minded thugs. But if they had a leader, if they had a figurehead, a boss-of-all-the-bosses, then it was Eamer.

Clar didn't actually think he'd be in the bar, holding court, accepting tributes. But they were relieved to see that he wasn't. The bar wasn't busy, although it was far from empty. Most of the clientele lurked in booths and shadows. Clar had no problem finding a stool at the bar.

The bartender was small and scruffy. She wore a grubby white shirt and an unbuttoned grey striped waistcoat. Her long hair was almost gathered into a hair band that was not up to the job.

She grabbed a glass from under the bar and flipped it upright, dropping it down onto the bar in front of Clar.

'Welcome, stranger!' she announced. 'What's your poison?'

Clar scanned the bottles behind the bar. Most of the labels were tattered, torn, and illegible.

'Vodka,' they said.

'Solid,' grinned the bartender, grabbing a bottle and filling it to the brim. 'Are you paying as you go, or do you want me to start a tab?'

Clar realised that, without their Com, their funds were limited. They stuck a hand in their coat to root for physical credits. They pulled out a note and a couple of coins.

'What will twenty three credits get me?'

The bartender raised her eyebrows and blew out a breath. Without saying a word, she picked up the glass from in front of Clar and took a swig.

'Not as much as was in that glass,' she gasped, hoarse from the burn.

'But the rest of it's mine?'

The bartender slid the cash off the bar and into her hand.

'All yours. Don't drink it all at once.'

Clar downed the rest of the oily liquid. It did burn. This was not high-quality alcohol.

'Don't tell me what to do,' they said.

Clar was pretty sure that they'd sounded unintentionally aggressive. They'd been going for flirtatious, but they hadn't pulled it off.

The bartender stuck out a hand. No offence had been taken.

'Mouse,' she said.

Clar wrinkled their brow with confusion. That didn't make sense.

'Me. My name,' insisted the bartender. 'I'm Mouse.'

'Right.'

Clar took the proffered hand and squeezed it. It was still an unfamiliar gesture to them, despite the time they'd spent in Trinity. They weren't sure it would ever feel comfortable.

'Clar Triebel.'

A slow smile spread across Mouse's face. She shook Clar's hand up and down with enthusiasm. Clar was taken aback. They felt like they'd met a new best friend that they weren't entirely sure they wanted.

'Clar Triebel,' repeated Mouse. 'Of all the bars in all of Trinity, you walked into mine.'

Clar got that chill, that creeping feeling of dread again. Who was this Mouse? A fan? Because they were talking like a stalker.

'You've heard of me?' they asked, as neutrally as they could.

'We have a mutual friend.'

Realisation dawned for Clar. Sim. Sim had said there was someone that they needed to meet. He had said little more than that. It was vague, even for Sim, and you got used to vague if you worked with him for long.

'Lagrange?' they checked.

Mouse's smile developed into a full grin as she finally dropped Clar's hand.

'The very man,' she confirmed. 'He's a father to me…'

Clar did a quick assessment. Jo Jo was in his early twenties. This woman had at least five years on him. What little she knew about Sim's past suggested a lack of long-term attachments.

'So you're Jo Jo's, what, half-sister?'

'Ew, no!' Mouse pulled a face of near disgust. 'No, not an actual father. I should have said *like* a father. Maybe an uncle. Or a slightly weird family friend. I don't know. I put that badly. Let me start again…'

She picked the vodka bottle up from the bar and refilled Clar's glass back up to the brim.

'This one's on Sim,' she explained. 'I'm sure he owes you a drink,'

She wasn't wrong. Clar raised the glass in a silent toast and drank it down. The burn was less, but the room spun a little more. It felt nice. Eamer's had seemed liked a terrifying place from afar. Now they were here, it was feeling a bit like home.

Mouse grabbed a second glass and poured herself a drink.

'I'll join you.' She glanced around the bar. 'There's no one in tonight who would disapprove of me drinking on the job and we have a lot to talk about.'

'You've got some catching up to do,' said Clar, opportunistically sliding their empty glass alongside Mouse's.

Mouse filled it for the third time, and they drank together.

By the time Fricker's runner, a street kid by the name of Sami, arrived, Clar had forgotten about their Com, and why they'd come to the bar in the first place. Mouse shooed Sami away with an air of someone who had to do so regularly, giving instructions to come back with the Com itself rather than demands for payment.

'Sim will cover that, too.' Her wink suggested that Lagrange himself wasn't aware of this arrangement.

Clar leaned back in their seat, feeling warm and safe and more at home than they had in years. Suddenly, leaving Trinity did not seem as attractive an option as it had a few hours before.

Maybe they could stay.

At the very least, they could give Sim the benefit of the doubt, see what Mouse had to show them. That, at least, would mean spending more time with Mouse, and that didn't seem like a bad thing.

'Do you eat anywhere else?' asked Konoroz, behind the counter. 'Not that I complain. We go out of business if not for you young, chaotic, unfussy people who do not care what they put into their bodies until it's too late.'

Clar looked at him askance. It felt like they were being criticised, but they weren't sure which adjective they took issue with.

'I'm not that young...' they mumbled, confusing themselves. *That wasn't the right one.*

They gripped the counter for balance, although it seemed to be covered in a sheen of grease that made that feel like a poor choice. Not holding on to something would be worse, though. They'd drunk a lot.

For the umpteenth time, they dipped their hand into the pocket of their overcoat. Their new ComN, freshly fixed by Fricker, as promised, sat at the bottom. As their fingers made contact, the strange message he'd given them played through their head again.

"We need you."

Who?

"All of us."

There came a cackle from behind them. Clar turned to see a wizened old man in a grey shawl. Konoroz's father often spent his evenings in the cafe he once ran, and it was still evening. Checking the time, it turned out it was still quite early evening. It was only Clar's advanced level of inebriation that was making it feel like the early hours of tomorrow.

'Good evening, sir,' they slurred.

'Good evening, not-so-young person,' grinned the elder. 'How goes the revolution?'

Clar sighed loudly, and with an exasperation that had been building for months. This was why they had had enough. This was why they could throttle Lagrange and his "you make a difference".

Why do I have to? Why always me?

They turned to face the old man, leaning back on the counter for badly needed support.

'No one cares!' they shouted, before adjusting their volume to a more conversational level. 'Everyone knows who Chaguartay is, what he is. He doesn't even try to hide it now. He lies, and he cheats and he has people attacked and killed and he takes everything he can from the people of this city...'

'Still, they vote for him,' agreed Konoroz Senior.

'Still, they vote for him. And they're going to do it again. The only explanation is that the vote is rigged, but even so... I worry. I worry people aren't thinking hard enough. I worry that even if it wasn't rigged, he'd still win... I worry that...'

'The people must be stupid...' said the old man.

'Yes! The people are stupid.'

The old man held up a hand, so Clar stopped talking.

'No, you misunderstand me,' he said. 'You think the people must be stupid. But they do not think like you. They do not think about the things you do...'

'But they must see that...' Clar cut in.

The old man flicked his wrist dismissively, and Clar fell quiet again.

'They do not see. They do not think about the things that you think about, and they do not think about the things you think they think about. They do not think about the things you think they *should* think about. They have their own perspectives and those perspectives are more important than

27

your mission to lift the veil and change their world.'

'But those needs would disappear if only we could change the world. That's the whole point!'

'It may be, but you have the luxury of being able to see the horizon. They do not know where they are. They do not see themselves as the lobsters in the pot, slowly being heated to the point of being boiled alive, because they've been pushed so far down that they can't see the edge of the pot…'

'And then there are the drugs in the water…' Konoroz Junior cut in.

'Tsk,' scoffed his father. 'Ignore my idiot son. He took no notice of the education I gave him. He talks like a simpleton and believes whatever it is he heard last. And his head is so far up his own arse that what he hears is mostly farts!'

The old man creased over as he was consumed by a cackling laugh that gave way too long, wheezing, hacking coughs.

'They…' Clar stopped before they got to their point, which had run away from them while they waited for Konoroz Senior to regain his breath.

He was right, though. Despite their best efforts, the vast majority of the people of Trinity had no idea how much trouble they were in. This was it. This was why they wanted to leave. Why wouldn't Lagrange just let them leave?

'I once knew a man,' continued Konoroz Senior. 'He moved into the apartment next to mine after the previous occupant passed away. He was so sickly. I would hear him moaning in the depths of night, shuddering wails that caused our paper-thin walls to flex and crack…'

Clar, even as drunk as they were, suspected that this was hyperbole, but the old man usually told a good story, so they let it pass. Konoroz slid an unwrapped kebab, oozing with garlic sauce and prickly with chilli, next to their elbow. Clar picked it up without taking their eyes off Konoroz Senior and hungrily sank their teeth in. The heady cocktail of grease, allium and capsaicin took them momentarily away to the place that only drunk people enjoying much anticipated food go, until the sound of the old man's voice brought them back into the shop.

'...I could take no more. Four months of my sleep had been taken from me, and I was not letting another night go. I hammered at his door until he opened it, slowly, peering at me with weak, squinting eyes. Immediately, the hot stench of rodent urine assaulted my senses. I took a step back and as the angle of my view of the apartment changed, I saw it there, in the middle of the hallway. A large, black rat sat on its hind legs regarding me. My neighbour did not know it was there.'

Clar nodded, slowly, silently, their mouth stuffed with kebab. They had never heard this story, but they knew how it ended.

'The man is the people,' explained Konoroz Senior.

Clar nodded more vigorously. They knew what the old man was asking.

'And Chaguartay is the rat.'

It was the same thing that Sim was asking.

Clar paid Konoroz, then tottered over to his father and planted a kiss on the old man's balding forehead. They picked up their kebab and walked back out into the night.

It wasn't that their mind had been made up. No one was giving them a choice, but that didn't matter. Clar knew there wasn't a choice to make.

CHAPTER 3

The doors of the vast freight elevator slid noisily open, revealing… nothing. Clar narrowed their eyes to peer into the gloom, but the bright lights of their carriage made it hard to see beyond the opening.

'Come on,' said Mouse, taking a long, heavy torch from somewhere inside her overcoat.

She shuffled towards the doorway, her oversized coat swishing across the floor as she moved. The figure she cut was scruffy and slightly ridiculous, but in the grimy, industrial setting of the lift, Clar felt far more inappropriately dressed in their business suit. They still weren't completely sure where they were being taken, but it was probable that a lower heel would have been desirable.

It wasn't their fault. They'd had to come straight from the Dome. The leader of Opposition, Jack White, had given a long and impassioned speech that protested the recent introduction of exit passes, effectively limiting the movement of Trinity residents out of the city. Clar had stayed to the end and did not have time to get home and change.

Mayor Chaguartay, of course, hadn't been in the chamber.

The speech, impressive and heartfelt as it was, would have no impact. Nothing ever did.

Despite this, Opposition believed, as a point of principle, they should continue to conduct politics as usual, to keep the apparatus of democracy alive and visible to the population. The mayor felt no such obligation. He'd sent a lackey, an aide, in his place. Ralph something. He'd sat and listened, taken notes and left.

Clar stepped out and, as their eyes adjusted to the grey half-light, they saw they were in a tunnel. The walls curved over their head, the ceiling low. They weren't quite able to bump their head on it, but it was close.

Along the ceiling ran what looked to be electrical cables, and there were double rails on the floor, like train tracks. They didn't get a good look at the walls before the lift doors closed, extinguishing the light and leaving only the strobe effect of Mouse flicking her torch back and forth.

'What are you doing?' asked Clar. 'You're giving me a headache.'

'Checking the coast is clear,' explained Mouse. 'You can never be too careful.'

'Careful of what, trains?' Clar's voice rose in panic. 'Isn't it best to check for those before you step out into the tunnel?'

'No, not trains,' scoffed Mouse, shining their torch back at Clar, apparently satisfied that whatever she had been looking for wasn't there. 'Haven't been trains for years.'

Clar shielded their eyes from the glare of the torchlight. Mouse was an employee of one of the worst people in Trinity. Who, exactly, was she worried about?

They'd learned a lot about Mouse in the intervening weeks. At least, they thought they had. It was hard to pinpoint anything super specific now they came to reflect, but it seemed she was rather more than a bartender. Mouse knew everyone and everyone knew Mouse. Mouse had a reputation for getting things done.

What things? Clar wasn't sure they wanted to know. They quite liked her, so far. In their experience, too much information often ruined a burgeoning friendship.

'I thought you worked for the Black Knights?' they pointed out.

'I work *with* the Black Knights,' Mouse clarified, 'and even that's complicated. Decentralised management structure, you know? It's hard to know where you stand sometimes. I work for Eamer, which gives me influence and a bit of extra leeway, but I'm really only a bartender as far as that's concerned. Anything else is on a… more freelance basis.'

'So you're saying that you can't talk your way out of it if we run into someone who's up to no good?'

'I'm saying I probably can't.'

'That probably amounts to the same thing.'

'Relax,' said Mouse, passing Clar and setting off up the tunnel. 'It's probably not going to be an issue.'

Clar turned and followed. They were right about their footwear being unsuitable. The floor between the rails was uneven and covered in debris and they had to pick their way, which wasn't easy while Mouse had her torch beam focused up ahead. It would be easier without the chunky heels, but there was no way they were taking them off. Some of the debris was squishy, and it didn't smell good.

'What are we doing here, anyway?' they called ahead to Mouse. 'In the dark, avoiding gangsters…'

'It's a surprise,' said Mouse, over her shoulder. 'We'll get to that. But isn't this place cool?'

Clar begged to differ, but they didn't say so.

'…so we ended up with three kilometres of tunnel running

between two stations. All underground, all completely useless.'

The tunnel was, it seemed, part of an abandoned project to move all of Trinity's public transport underground.

'And this was all Chaguartay's idea?' asked Clar.

'It was part of his big push for election, first time around,' said Mouse. 'Move all the transport underground, then turn the surface into a pedestrian's paradise. Green spaces, clean air…'

'That seems rather more progressive than I've found him to be. It sounds like a good idea.'

'Well, it all depends on your perspective…'

There was a faint light up ahead, where the tunnel bent away to the left. A red glow pulsed in the distance.

'And what's your perspective?'

'I don't think he ever had any intention of completing the project,' said Mouse. 'He can plead naïve enthusiasm all he likes, but he knew it couldn't work. We all knew, and he told us it didn't matter and we all believed him because we wanted what he was promising. Trinity is built on sand. Sand and bog, and a massive great plague pit.'

'That doesn't sound… stable?'

'It's not. Most of the excavations collapsed. There are tunnelling shields buried all over the city. They just couldn't get them out. It might have worked if they'd dug deeper, but… it would have had to be really deep. Then there was this place.'

They'd reached the corner. The pale red glow was bright enough to light their way now, but Clar thought they'd preferred it when they couldn't see where they were putting their feet. There were definitely rats on the tunnel floor, both alive and dead.

Mouse was climbing a set of stone steps at the edge of the tunnel, and Clar followed her up to a narrow ledge which led around the corner.

'Welcome,' said Mouse, 'to Citadel station. Although, of course, it's nowhere near the Citadel because that would have involved tunnelling through The Catacombs, which would have brought the whole thing crashing to the ground.'

They found themselves on a long, narrow platform, which curved around to the right, following the shape of the tunnel. The walls were lined with cream-coloured tiles, interspersed with splashes of colour. Further down, there appeared to be a giant mosaic depicting the round head of a middle-aged, balding man with cauliflower ears and a squashed nose.

'Our esteemed mayor,' chuckled Mouse, pointing at it from down the platform. 'It's not the most flattering depiction. I mean, he's not exactly a handsome man, but even I feel sorry for him when I look at that.'

Clar read the words underneath the mural.

'Chaguartay Line? Is that what it's called?'

'It's what it was meant to be called,' replied Mouse. 'These days it's just known as The Drain.'

'Because of the waste of money?' Clar hazarded.

'Because of all the crap that washes down it.'

Overhead, there were signs and dead electronic displays, casting long shadows in the red emergency lighting. Along the length of the platform, there were several metal benches, litter bins and a vending machine with the door hanging open.

While Clar watched, a rat plopped out of the machine and scampered over the yellow line that ran the length of the platform. It took a running jump, launching itself off the edge and down into the unseen gap between the tracks.

'What are we doing here?' asked Clar, again.

'Right now? Mouse's magical mystery tour! I thought you'd be interested to see the hidden side of the city. It's quite something, isn't it?'

Clar had to admit that they were, in a way, enjoying themselves. They were getting to experience a Mouse-eye view of this strange city, that they'd travelled so far and waited so long to reach, and had been on the verge of giving up on.

Mouse was good company, simultaneously warm and approachable, but also enigmatic and with a tendency to push you back to arm's length if you got too close. That wasn't a criticism. Clar would admit to having an idiosyncratic personality themselves. If anything, they found it reassuring.

It was people who seemed completely open who were the most suspicious. Everyone, Clar had learned the hard way, had something to hide. If someone seemed like they didn't, then they were too good at hiding it to be trusted.

There was a low rumble down the tunnel, from the direction that they had come up to the station. A shift in the air, a heat rolling up towards them, the vibrations under their feet. Something was coming.

'Is that all we're here for?' asked Clar, cautiously. 'I thought you said there weren't any trains?'

They were quite prepared to revisit their earlier assessment. They cursed themselves for not taking better precautions. If Mouse was about to reveal that she had led them into a trap, they were exposed right now. Not that they didn't back themselves to fight themselves out of a tricky corner, but it did all depend on who was coming up the tunnel. And how many of them there were.

'We need to hide,' hissed Mouse, running across to the broken vending machine and pulling at the side.

It easily swung out from the wall, revealing a small nook, a hole in the brickwork behind the large metal box. Clar hesitated. Everything they'd just processed still held. They didn't know Mouse that well and there were no guarantees that she wasn't going to doublecross them. Climbing into a hole in the wall with her wasn't necessarily the best plan.

The best plan probably wasn't available right now, though, and Clar thought any plan was better than no plan. They squeezed themselves into the hole next to Mouse and, gripping the side of the vending machine, they swung it mostly closed.

The train, when it arrived, was just the one carriage and an engine. Four robed figures jumped out. They seemed to be dressed in purple, in the red of the emergency lighting, but Clar has seen similar robes before and, if this was who they thought it was, they were usually blue.

'Devoted?' They were shocked.

Mouse didn't react, hadn't reacted to the Clerics' appearance, hadn't reacted to Clar's shock. They were squashed closely enough together in the hole in the wall for Clar to tell. They could almost feel her pulse.

'I can't see,' hissed Mouse. 'But they're not Devoted.'

'You seem pretty certain.'

'Do they have full heads of hair?'

The men - and Clar was pretty sure they were all men - heavyset figures rumbling indistinct syllables did, indeed, possess full heads of hair. The monotone of their grunt settled into a rhythm as they began heaving crates from the carriage and stacking them against the wall of the platform.

'See, not Clerics,' said Mouse, apparently satisfied that Clar would have come to the same conclusion.

'What are they doing?'

'Driving an out-of-service train up a disused tunnel in the middle of the night? Bringing unmarked crates from Docklands up to the Citadel, disguised as Clerics?'

'Smugglers?' hazarded Clar.

'Bingo,' said Mouse. 'This is what I wanted to show you. This is what we are doing here…'

The crates multiplied against the wall. Each was light enough to be carried by one man, and their journey back and forth to the carriage was short. Four, eight, twelve... twenty four... forty eight... in a matter of minutes, they'd finished, and all disappeared back into the carriage.

'Are they just going to leave them there?' asked Clar.

They thought they got it, now. They thought they understood. The smugglers were going to store the crates in this abandoned place, deep under the street, lost and forgotten. They would be safe here. No one would suspect.

Except for Mouse. Mouse had connections, Mouse knew people, Mouse could get a good price. They were going to have to make a choice. If Mouse was determined to rob these people, then Clar had to decide if they were in or out. This was a test, an initiation. Mouse had taken a shine to Clar. They could tell that. There was a price for that, too.

Clar had done what they had to, in the past, to survive. The journey from Rosaan, the six months camped in the Armpit of the Northern Exposure... They weren't innocent, they weren't squeaky clean. Sim knew about all of it.

Sim had to know about this too, and if he was behind it, then it wasn't a *crime*, as such. It had to be some kind of redistribution effort, or a way of destabilising a Black Knight gang. They just wished he'd been open with them. The secrecy unnerved them.

The men emerged from the carriage again, this time carrying a larger crate. If the effort it seemed to take was anything to go by, it was significantly heavier, too. They only just managed to drag it out. It took all four of them to lift it over the gap between the carriage and the platform.

Halfway across to the stack of smaller crates, they gave up, and let it crash to the ground. The sound reverberated around the enclosed space, prompting nervous glances all around to check that no one had heard.

'Idiots,' muttered Mouse. 'Handle with care.'

Clar wondered what was in the final crate. Mouse obviously knew.

The smugglers climbed back into the engine and it noisily backed down the tunnel, the way they had come. Clar and Mouse waited until the silence had resettled before they felt safe enough to emerge from their hiding place. There was a chill to the air, Clar noticed, now that they were not huddled next to Mouse.

'So how does this work?' Clar asked. 'You walk a crate back up to the elevator? How many do we take?'

'What?'

She looked genuinely confused, but Clar assumed they had been unclear, rather than that they were mistaken.

'You're taking this, right? How does it work? Do you sell it on yourself? Or do you have a connection in the Knights?'

'What the…? Clar, those *were* the Black Knights. What are you talking about?'

'Those were…? But don't you work for the Black Knights?'

Mouse sighed noisily, reaching into her overcoat and this time taking out a short metal bar.

'We've been through this,' she scolded, placing the flattened end of the metal bar between the top and the side of the crate.

'Hold on, did you just happen to bring your own crowbar?'

It must have been tucked away in Mouse's coat all this time, and yet Clar hadn't felt a thing while they'd been squashed into their hiding place.

'You're asking about all the wrong details,' growled Mouse.

'I'm a journalist,' retorted Clar. 'There are no wrong details.'

'Fine.' Mouse prised the lid away from the crate and stood

back.

Clar moved towards the gap that Mouse had created and peered inside. After a moment, their eyes adjusted and they could see what was curled inside the crate. There, on a bed of straw, apparently asleep, was a young woman. She looked like she could use a good meal, but otherwise, she seemed healthy and unharmed. Apart from being asleep at the bottom of a crate.

'Is she OK?' asked Clar, unable to think of a less stupid question.

'Once the drugs wear off, she'll be OK,' replied Mouse. 'Or she will be if you can get her out of here.'

'Me?' asked Clar.

Not that they didn't want to help, but this wasn't what they'd expected.

'It's like I said,' said Mouse, looking nervous, vulnerable for the first time. 'I work with the Black Knights, and that makes things complicated. I have to be careful what I say, who I say it to. But you're not part of this. You're not even from Trinity. If you knew something, if you saw something, it would be the most natural thing in the world for you to help...'

Clar looked into Mouse's pleading eyes, and they understood. They'd almost got Mouse wrong. This was who she was.

As the tears broke and flowed down Mouse's face, Clar folded her in their arms, and together, in the darkness, they made their plan

CHAPTER 4

'Her name is Hana,' said Clar to Sim, several days later, back in their flat.

Sim had stopped by for a beer while Clar was having their morning coffee. It seemed he'd been up all night, so this wasn't necessarily a red flag, but there wasn't really any telling with Sim.

Hana, the girl from the crate, was asleep in Clar's bed. Clar had spent the last few nights on the sofa, and was feeling that fact in their lower back. They didn't know how Jo Jo had stuck it out for as long as he had.

'Why'd you bring her here?' asked Sim.

He appeared to be on edge but, again, there wasn't really any telling. He often appeared to be on edge.

It was a stupid question. Where else were they supposed to take her?

'The trafficked woman depot was closed,' they replied.

'Oh, OK, OK.' Sim put his beer down. 'I'm sorry. I get Mouse didn't leave you with a lot of choice. That wasn't really the question I was trying to ask. I mean, why you? Why not Mouse? She has the connections. I didn't really mean for you to get this involved. I just thought you should have the story.'

'She seemed scared. She seemed to think she needed to keep her distance.'

'Yeah,' Sim rubbed his face, swept up his beer, took a long swig. 'That's what I was afraid you were going to say. She didn't tell me she was scared.'

Clar didn't think that telling people she was scared was the sort of thing Mouse did, especially not when the person concerned was Sim. She hadn't even told Clar she was scared. She'd just said that she couldn't get involved. And then burst into tears.

Clar had no choice but to get involved in her stead.

'So you just scooped her out of the box and carried her up the stairs?' asked Sim.

It had been less elegant, involved a bit more messy stumbling, but essentially, that was correct.

'Pretty much.' Clar wouldn't let on. It didn't hurt to impress him. 'Up through the Catacombs, out of the Citadel gates. Then back here. She barely stirred until yesterday afternoon. I don't know what they gave her...'

Sim shivered. Clar was always surprised at his reaction to even the mention of pharmaceutical drugs. For such a dedicated alcoholic, he was quite selective about what he was prepared to put into his body.

'That must have taken a lot of strength,' he said.

Clar shrugged. They would not deny it. The girl was thin, there was hardly anything to her, but moving from the depths of the underground tunnel to the surface was a significant gain in elevation. There had also been several miles of Catacomb they'd had to negotiate.

'I broke a sweat,' they admitted modestly.

'Where's she from?'

'Øp, I think, or somewhere in that region. Øp adjacent... I

don't know, Reznikia or maybe even one of the desert states? I don't know the dialect...'

That did trouble Clar. They considered themselves well travelled, but this girl's vocabulary was peppered with words that were completely alien to them. Still, they'd each managed to make themselves understood well enough to prepare and share a meal the previous night. It had been a pleasant evening. Clar suspected they had a lot in common.

'We should probably decide what we're doing with her.' Sim finished his beer and tossed the bottle into the recycling. 'It's not safe for either of you if she stays here much longer. There will be Knights out looking for her. You're far enough out of the darker parts of town that it will take them a while to find you, but... well, it's already been a while and they *will* find you.'

'I don't think we should do anything *with* her,' objected Clar. 'I think we should let her recover and then see what she wants.'

Sim rubbed his face again. He stood up from his chair and walked the short distance to the kitchen. Clar heard the fridge door open and close, heard the bottle cap prised from another beer, heard the glug and the sigh from Sim.

Sim's drinking was like water being poured over hot coals. Too much would have put out the flames, killed the heat. But Sim knew just how much was needed to get the steam rising, raise the temperature, get things really going. He just kept pouring at that rate, and all anyone around him could do was to sweat.

Clar suspected they were about to get a full blast. He stood in the doorway, his jaw grinding. Clar knew that look. He didn't agree. Well, they hadn't expected him to and, to be frank, *fuck him*. This wasn't about him.

'I get what you're saying,' he muttered, eventually. 'I really do, and she should have that right. Of course she should. But I think we need to be pragmatic here. She can't just do whatever she wants…'

'Yes, she can,' insisted Clar. 'We can warn her it's a bad idea, but she can absolutely decide to do whatever she chooses. Including walking out of here, heading back down through The Catacombs to Citadel station and climbing back into that crate.'

Sim looked stumped.

'That's a metaphor, right?' he checked.

'Maybe.'

They hadn't meant it as one, but they had no problem with Sim thinking that they had. Especially not if it stopped him from deciding people's lives for them.

He did that, Clar realised. He did that to them. Always for the greater good, always for the right reasons, but almost everything they'd done over the last four years had, in some way, been Sim's idea.

Sim always did everything for the right reasons. But he had the certainty of a locomotive and could plough through anything that found itself in his way, logic and humanity included. Not that he didn't care. He just didn't see it.

That was what was happening now. *Well, no more.*

'We wait,' they said. 'We wait, we ask, and we help her. On her terms, not ours. Not yours.'

Clar was certain this was heading for an escalating confrontation, so Sim's smile was unexpected. It broke, creasing his usually sagging features, splitting across his face. Clar realised they hadn't really understood the phrase "grinning from ear to ear" until now.

'Perfect,' he said. 'No notes. That's what we'll do.'

Deflated, Clar knew it had happened again. They'd just walked straight into Sim's trap.

'What are you playing at?' they asked the dumb, grinning agent in front of them.

'I'm sorry.' Sim's his face softened, or at least lost some of the manic edge. 'I didn't mean to trick you, but I didn't know how else to… I don't think you'd have accepted it if I'd just told you.'

He moved back into the narrow living room and fell back into the armchair. Clar shifted uneasily on the sofa. They had a feeling they were about to be taught a lesson. They had a feeling that their pride would not find it a comfortable experience.

'We need you,' said Sim, more gently. 'We can't do this without you. Regardless of where she came from, originally, Hana was in the same camp you were, out in the Armpit. You've been on the same journey, you just took different paths. You got brought in by Opposition, because they thought you'd be useful to their cause. She got brought in by the Black Knights because they thought she'd be useful to their profits. But you're both here now. And no one understands what she needs right now like you do.'

Clar's eyes pricked with tears that they really didn't want to cry. Not now, not here, not in front of Sim. Not while there was work to do. Because he was a shit and he was full of himself. But he was right.

'That's why I need to stay.' Clar's voice was barely a whisper.

'I'm sorry,' said Sim again, shifting over to the sofa and putting an arm around Clar's shoulders. 'But yes, it is.'

Mouse flipped two glasses onto the bar and filled them. Clar hadn't paid for a drink in Eamer's since that first night. Apparently, it wasn't necessary once you were a friend of Mouse.

Clar had protested the excessive generosity. Mouse had protested that any generosity was involved. It wasn't, she said, like she was picking up the tab, which gave Clar reason to question the accounting practices at Eamer's, and why he cared so little whether his takings bore any relation to his sales.

There was a story there, but it was more Sim's field than theirs. They weren't interested in Eamer. They kept coming because it turned out that Eamer's wasn't only the haunt of gangsters and assassins. Significant political figures also seemed to be fond of living it down around the docks.

'What's he doing?' hissed Clar, as Mouse poured.

'He's sitting.' Mouse glanced over Clar's shoulder. 'But he's looking this way, so don't turn around. We'll just have a nice little drink together, over here, and as soon as I spot who he's meeting, I'll let you know.'

Clar sipped their vodka carefully. They needed a straight head on tonight. They had a feeling that things might be about to move quickly and they needed to be on their toes.

Behind them, in the booth, sat Jack White, mayoral candidate and leader of Opposition. He wore a peaked cap, pulled down to cover his eyes, and several days of beard growth. It wasn't enough to obscuring the instantly recognisable visage, familiar from his campaign videos and media appearances.

It was undeniably him, just as it had been undeniably him every other time he'd lurked in the corner of this and several other bars, under Clar's supervision, over the past few months.

'Well, we know it won't be Manukan, at least,' said Clar, grimly.

Jack White's drinking companions varied, but Ralph Manukan had been a regular associate. Which was strange because Manukan worked for Chaguartay. Clar would have loved to know what they discussed. There was a story *there*, they knew it.

Maybe there wasn't any more. Because last week Ralph Manukan had turned up in an alley with a bullet in his back.

'You know that's now Sim's case?'

'I did,' confirmed Clar. 'Doesn't make sense, though. It couldn't have been Black Knights.'

'It looked like Black Knights…'

'It wasn't, though. They enjoy too much of the mayor's favour to put that at risk by bumping off his right-hand man.'

'I think "right-hand man" might be pushing it.'

Mouse could scoff, but Clar wasn't so sure. They'd heard stories. Gossip, rumours, sure, but the same ones, many times, from many people. They couldn't easily discount them.

'Maybe if Manukan did something to piss his boss off…'

'Like what?'

'I'm working on that. Is he still on his own?'

Clar finished sipping. Their glass was empty. Mouse refilled it, nodding with subtlety.

'He's just ordered from Kashka,' she said. 'You want me to slip something into it?'

Kashka was a server at Eamer's. Quite a cute one. Clar was very fond of her. As was Jo Jo. Not that they were in competition.

'No,' Clar would not stoop to drugging their quarry.

'Might make him more inclined to talk…?'

'No.'

There was a silence. Mouse moved some glasses around, picked the bottle up, put it back down again. She was fidgeting, edgy.

'We just need to wait,' said Clar. 'Go serve someone else. You're making me nervous. He'll see that you're watching him in a moment and then the whole thing's ruined.'

Mouse moved away, busied herself with other customers.

Clar shuffled around in their seat and looked about. If they were careful about it they could risk turning, getting a look at Jack White themselves.

His head was bowed. He was three booths away from where Clar perched at the bar, but there was no one in those, so they got a clear view of the top of his cap. They couldn't see what he was looking at, though, down on the table. It could have been his Com, but Clar had an impression that it was something else, something more basic, more analogue.

They couldn't see what, though. A book? A card? A message scrawled on a napkin? They turned back to their drink, and Mouse reappeared.

'Keep watching, see if you can see what's so interesting on the table…'

'So where's Hana?' asked Mouse, without taking her eyes off the booth over Clar's shoulder. 'It's strange to see you without your shadow.'

Clar winced. They didn't want to talk about that. A lot had happened in a short space of time, too much to tell Mouse at the time, too much to fill her in on now. It would hurt too much. Clar wasn't proud of very much of what they'd done.

What Hana had wanted, it turned out, involved something that Clar wasn't able to give her. They hadn't handled it well.

'She's gone,' they said.

She hadn't gone, not in any of the senses that Mouse would have understood that sentence. But that was too much to talk about, here and now. It was more than Clar could figure out how to explain.

They weren't used to explaining. Jo Jo apart - and that was purely casual - they'd spent a long time on their own, either actually on their own, or alone in a sea of people who didn't have their best interests at heart. Like in the Armpit. The camps took a long time to shake off, it seemed.

Camps or no camps, Mouse was still new in their life. It would take her time to win Clar's complete trust. That was just how it was. Which was convenient, because they really didn't want to talk about Hana.

Hana had been new in their life. Now she wasn't.

Mouse straightened up.

'What?'

Clar attempted to lock eyes with her, but she continued to stare over their shoulder, gaze fixed on White's booth. Clar didn't dare turn around, but they needed to know.

'Who?' they demanded. 'Who is it?'

Mouse laughed without tearing her eyes away.

'I mean,' she said. 'This is probably one of the least suspicious people that man could meet with. This could be nothing.'

Clar continued to stare at Mouse. There was nowhere else they could look. But they didn't understand what she was getting at.

'Who? I swear to the Dear Creator, you need to tell me what's going on, Mouse...'

'On the other hand, given where they're meeting, and that they're both obviously trying to pretend to be anyone other than who they actually are...'

'Fuck's sake Mouse...'

Mouse tore her gaze away and looked back at Clar.

'You're never going to guess...' she teased.

Clar grabbed her by the bowtie. Mouse stuck her hands, a picture of wide-eyed innocence.

'All right, all right, calm down,' she said. 'But you will not believe this. It's his wife.'

Clar spun around and stared. Mouse was right, that was Evie White.

Evie White was rarely seen in public. She kept a low profile, out of necessity.

Because Evie White was not just Jack White's wife, not just a significant player in Opposition, not just suspected of being the true power behind the man standing against the incumbent mayor.

Evie White was Stam Chaguartay's daughter.

CHAPTER 5

The first time that Authority Cadet Shalini Parker came to Clar's flat, they didn't let her in. Just because they had a working relationship with Sim, didn't mean that they had trust in Authority in a general sense.

Sim had not been in touch for days, anyway. Clar was annoyed at him.

The second time that Authority Cadet Shalini Parker came to Clar's flat, they didn't let her in. She wasn't fooling anyone.

Sim was a friend. Sim had vanished. Everyone was a suspect as far as Clar was concerned.

Clar was certainly suspicious of this Parker. Parker was probably suspicious of Clar. That was also a worry. She appeared to know where Clar lived. Maybe this was the time to get out of town after all.

There was too much unfinished business, though. The smuggling investigation, and Sim's work on the Manukan murder, for a start. Sim's disappearance. Jo Jo. Hana. Mouse.

Clar kicked themselves for getting so involved. Not so long ago, it would have been easy to leave, to remove themselves with minimal wrench, minimal effort. How had they allowed themselves to put down roots so firmly that the pain of leaving scared them more than the risk of staying?

The third time that Authority Cadet Shalini Parker came to Clar's flat, they let her in, because they'd lost the strength to keep her at arm's length. Trinity was threatening to bury them alive. It seemed easier just to let it.

Parker sat at Clar's kitchen table nursing a mug of tea, which had long since gone cold. The conversation seemed to have ground to a halt.

Comparing notes, neither of them had any idea where Sim might have gone. Both of them had searched everywhere they could think of, neither of them believed he would have left Trinity.

He'd said nothing, done nothing suspicious, or at least nothing that was any more suspicious than his regular behaviour. The last time that either of them had heard from him, on the night that he disappeared, he'd been with Mouse.

But Mouse knew nothing. They'd both interrogated her, informally and with varying levels of alcoholic input. She'd been consistent in her story that she'd left him deep in The Alleys. Mouse had been cagey about what she'd been doing deep in The Alleys, but Clar had got a vague admission that she'd been running messages for Resistance, which Parker seemed to think would check out.

Mouse seemed to be well known within Authority. Mouse was well known everywhere.

'You think that's the whole story?' asked Parker, looking up from her tea.

'From Mouse? You'll never get the whole story.' Clar was leaning back against the sink, observing the Authority agent. 'For what it's worth, I don't think she's hiding anything. Not intentionally, anyway…'

Parker's look intensified.

'What do you mean by that? You think she's hiding something unintentionally? Like she's forgotten?'

Clar hadn't meant to share this detail. But they realised how much it had been bothering them, and saying it out loud, they made a connection. They were surprised they hadn't made it earlier.

'Yes, like some of that night has been blanked out,' they said, and now they knew it was true. 'Which is strange, because when I try to think back...'

'You can't remember it either?' Parker finished their sentence for them.

'Yes. I feel like I can remember everything from moment to moment. There aren't any gaps in my timeline. Everything flows, everything makes logical, sequential, chronological sense but...'

'But there's something missing? Something you can't see?'

'Something in between the moments,' said Clar, feeling stupid as they did.

What could possibly be between the moments?

'I know exactly what you mean,' said Parker.

At night, from up there, Ashuana City barely looked real. On the fifty-second floor, higher than any of the neighbouring blocks, everything was at a distance, one step removed.

People were buried in the blackness below. The farthest thing he could see were the lights of the boxy vehicles, flowing like components on a production line. Here and there were rooftops that were more than tile and concrete - a roof garden, an infinity pool - but those seemed to be no more than images, as if seen on a Com screen from afar.

He felt no more connection with them as the bright lights of Exchange Plaza, far in the distance, nearer the river. Even those towers seemed shrunk and insignificant compared to his towering presence.

It was quiet on the executive floor. Everyone had left to go to their homes and their families and other places that he didn't care to go. He wasn't working though, not this late. He wasn't that kind of CEO. He believed in getting other people to do the work, so that he could watch it all function.

Like machinery.

Like the traffic below him.

He watched everything. He saw everything.

There was, however, one piece of business left to attend to. It had to be done when there was nobody else around. He heard the door to his office swish behind him. Just what he was waiting for, precisely on time.

Thurstan Beck Senior turned around to face the doorway.

'Christopher,' he said to the new arrival. 'Please, take a seat.'

'Thank you, sir,' said the man. 'Please, call me Crispy. Only my mother calls me Christopher, y'know.'

Thurstan Beck cringed inwardly, but did not betray himself.

What a ghastly name, for a ghastly man, he thought.

'Of course,' he agreed, determined that he would not use it. 'Thank you for coming to see me.'

'Of course.' Christopher "Crispy" Burton sat down in the chair in front of the wide desk, adjusting his ridiculous waistcoat as he sat.

Beck took his own seat, which was positioned to be several inches higher. He looked down at his sales executive. Burton seemed ill at ease, which pleased him. It was always difficult when you put as much trust in a man as he had done with Christopher Burton. They had a tendency to take it as a mark of your respect and esteem. They could get above themselves, decide that they were rather more important to you than they actually were.

That usually came just before they learned things they might use against you. It was time to make sure Christopher Burton knew his place.

'Tell me,' smiled Beck. 'How are the contract negotiations going with Trinity Administration?'

Burton shifted uneasily in his seat. Beck enjoyed watching him squirm. He enjoyed watching anyone squirm, but Burton did it particularly well.

'There...' Burton paused, weighing up his thoughts, trying to figure out what the right answer was. 'There aren't any contract negotiations taking place with Trinity Administr...'

Beck watched as the penny dropped. He was right, of course. There weren't any contract negotiations taking place with Trinity Administration. That wasn't what Burton had been making several years' worth of monthly visits to Trinity to discuss.

TrakcD Solutions, Beck's highly successful, internationally respected software business, could, of course, be in negotiations with the Trinity government to provide its services. It would make sense. Trinity was rich, and TrakcD made very good software.

Correction: there was a lot of money in Trinity. Trinity wasn't rich.

Regardless, that wasn't what Burton was doing. Beck had personal business interests in Trinity, which Burton had been looking after. They weren't as legitimate as software. Trinity wasn't the most legitimate place.

There was a lot of money in Trinity. Beck liked to help himself.

'I've had word,' continued Beck, 'from people who would know these things that your most recent visit has been noticed.'

'Noticed?' Burton looked shocked. 'Noticed by whom?'

He had a stammer when he was rattled. Beck remembered that now. He also dropped the affected mode of speech. Beck found him altogether less irritating when he was on the defensive. It worked that way, for him, with most people, to be fair.

'It doesn't matter.' Beck cut him down. 'But you've overstepped. We need to claw this back. How do you think we should do that?'

Burton looked lost. Beck could see his eyes flicking back and forth, searching his memory for a clue, for a moment that he made a mistake, blew his cover. Beck knew he would not find one. That wasn't why they were having this conversation.

'Let me help,' he said, because he was getting bored and he had dinner reservations. 'I think it's time that we opened negotiations with Trinity Administration.'

The relief that flooded Burton's face was palpable. Suddenly, the confidence returned. He sat up straight, tugged the creases back out of the waistcoat.

'Well, of course, sir,' he said, brightly, all trace of his stammer evaporating. 'Say no more. I'll get right on the overnight and commence negotiations sharpish. We'll have a contract on your desk before you can say "knife", rah?'

He mispronounced "knife" as "kerniffey". Beck assumed it was deliberate, but that only made him cringe harder. He didn't try very hard to hide it this time.

'I don't know that's a good idea,' said Beck. 'I don't think that you should set foot in Trinity for a while. Not until...'

'Until...' asked Burton.

Beck considered whether this was information he was prepared to share. He hadn't planned to.

'Is there something I should know? If I've compromised you, or our arrangements, in any way, I'm truly, deeply...'

Beck didn't have time for the hand wringing. He needed to shut this down. Steak. He thought he'd have steak. Not even the synthesised stuff. Actual beef.

'You will be aware, Christopher...'

'Crispy, please,' Burton corrected him.

'Christopher,' insisted Beck. He'd had enough. 'You will be aware that Trinity is currently preparing for elections. Elections that the incumbent mayor, Stam Chaguartay, is widely expected to win.'

Burton nodded. He knew this, everyone knew this. Every knew that Chaguartay would rig the election and be returned as mayor by a landslide, further strengthening his hold on the city and everything that happened inside those walls.

Thurstan Beck knew everyone was wrong.

'I think Trinity may be about to experience an unexpected period of instability.'

'Instability?' Burton looked further confused. 'You mean like... regime change?'

Beck laughed.

'That's a strong way of putting it. But yes.'

The words hung in the air between the two men, floating in the silence while Burton's jaw flapped soundlessly.

'But... how?' he asked, eventually.

'Doesn't matter.' Beck stood up. 'I have it on good authority. I don't think you should take your usual trip this month, and I think it would be a good idea for us to strengthen our alibi for any future meetings.'

Burton rose to his feet as well. The waistcoat rode up. He tugged it down.

'So you want me to open negotiations?'

'No,' Beck shook his head. 'I think we should send someone else. Someone more junior. Someone who can make the contact we need, with no risk of actually striking a deal that we don't really want.'

Burton paused, confusion creasing his face again.

'So you don't want to actually make a deal?' he checked.

'No,' said Beck. 'Only to appear to try to make one. If we made a deal, then we'd actually have to supply Trinity Administration. Which I don't want to do.'

'You don't?'

This was becoming tiresome. Beck was regretting ever having involved Burton in his Trinity project. He did it so well, though. It called for exactly the blend of smarm, cocksurity and barely justified confidence that made him the perfect front for the less legitimate side of Beck's portfolio.

'I don't,' he confirmed. 'I want us to look like we're trying, but I definitely do not want us to succeed. There is money to be made in Trinity, but that money is well away from the bureaucratic nightmare that passes for its government departments. We should choose our representative very carefully.'

'Someone we can reliably take into our confidence,' mused Burton. 'They'll need to be ambitious. Unprincipled. Fond of a vice that requires rather more funds than they currently have access to. Helincourt?'

Beck almost wavered. Helincourt would be an excellent choice, for all the reasons that Burton had just listed. He'd also be a terrible choice, because he wouldn't do it if they didn't tell him why, which would mean diluting the profits that he was already having to share with Burton.

They needed someone that they could guarantee wouldn't strike a deal, through his own natural incompetence and inadequacy. Someone who wasn't up for the job. Ideally, someone who would bunk off for the day, find a bar, get himself hopelessly drunk and miss the last train home.

'I thought Estrel might be the perfect candidate,' he said.

Estrel. His, Thurstan Beck's, son. Not his only son, not his favourite son, but his flesh and blood, nonetheless. He'd weighed the pros and cons of this approach. Not at length, but he'd weighed them.

Thurstan Beck was not a paternal man.

'Are you sure, sir?' asked Burton, aghast.

'You don't think it's a good idea?'

Beck wasn't really interested in Burton's opinion because he didn't value it. He was interested to see how far the man would go to dissuade him, though. He didn't think that Burton had the balls. He would have to think about what he would do about it if it turned out that he did.

'I mean, I guess…' Burton seemed to consider his words. 'If you think he's up to… It's not that he's a bad salesman necessarily…'

'He is a bad salesman,' said Beck.

It was true. That was one reason he wanted to send him.

'That's not really want I meant,' Burton backtracked. 'It's more that… I don't think his heart's in it.'

That was the other reason.

'He's perfect.' Beck moved towards the doorway, ushering Burton in the same direction. *Steak with a truffle butter.* 'But it shouldn't come from me.'

Burton stopped in the doorway.

'You want me to tell him?' he seemed reluctant.

Don't tell me no. It will not be good for you to tell me no.

'I think it would sound better coming from you. Someone senior, someone he aspires to be. Well, someone he should aspire to be. If I ask him, he'll say no.'

I'm not sure that he would say no. I don't think he even has that in him.

Nobody else would dare to say no.

'I mean…'

59

Burton looked pleased. Beck didn't think he needed to worry about Burton. Burton was right where he needed him to be. Just as Estrel would be, very soon.

'I'm sure you'll be very persuasive,' he said, shoving Burton the rest of the way through the door.

'Oh, yes, thanks, OK.' Burton turned as the door was closing. 'I'll do the necessary. Estrel will be on the next train to...'

Beck didn't hear the rest of it through the closed door. There was probably a "rah" at the end. He marched to the far side of the office and took his private lift to the parking garage.

The lift was fast, but there were a lot of floors to cover. He took his Com from his pocket and composed a brief message. Satisfied, he sent it.

Hundreds of miles away, in Trinity, Mayor Stam Chaguartay's Com beeped in receipt of another notification. He ignored it. Where was the boy?

It was taking a while to get used to having family around. Apart from Sara, and Sara didn't count, he'd held his family at arm's length. Ever since his wife died, since Evie distanced herself, for ten years he'd been an island, surrounded by sycophants and yes-men.

Everything had changed in a matter of months.

It wasn't just the gap left by Manukan's murder, the actual practical need to replace someone he relied upon more than anyone really knew. It was the uncomfortable realisation that he had vulnerabilities. Now, everyone could see that it was possible to strike at the heart of his empire; it was possible to wound him.

He'd trusted Manukan, and Manukan had been a flawed man. He would not make that mistake again. Pallis was his sister's boy. He would have been brought up right. She wouldn't have stood for any deviancy. Traditional vices only.

Chaguartay shouted the boy's name, and he appeared in the doorway.

'You need something, boss?'

Chaguartay nodded. It had taken a while to stop calling him "Uncle" at the end of every sentence. Chaguartay hadn't wanted to advertise the fact that he was drafting distant relatives onto his staff. He felt it highlighted that aforementioned vulnerability.

'Pills,' he said.

Again, vulnerability. That was the other factor that had changed his thinking. His illness was advanced. They hadn't picked it up early enough. He needed to fix things, prepare the ground for when he wasn't around anymore.

Pallis disappeared to collect the pills. Chaguartay pulled the next document up on his Com tablet. A request for an interview. He hadn't heard of the journalist. It looked like they were from outside, working for a channel in Rosaan, of all places.

Good people, the Rosaanans. Respected a strong leader. Knew their place, appreciated the value of someone who knew what was best for them. He'd go down well in Rosaan, he thought. He might not even have to resort to bribery and corruption to make his point.

Maybe he'd come to the wrong place. Maybe Trinity had been the wrong plan. It was the plan he made, though.

Now he was dying. He had little choice but to see it through.

He tapped at his screen, logged a ticket from the interview request. Call it ego, but he thought he'd enjoy doing it. He was going to say "yes".

Pallis stumbled back into his office and plonked the pill pot on his desk.

'Thank you,' he barked. 'I've just sent you an appointment ticket. See to it, please.'

The boy nodded enthusiastically and bounded off to do his bidding. Pallis was basically a puppy. Perhaps it hadn't been the best plan to bring him in. Chaguartay wasn't sure he had the steel he'd need for when things got tough. Not that would matter, not for much longer.

He picked up his Com from the desk and checked the earlier notification. A message from Ashuana City. Good news, as well. Maybe it wasn't all too late for him. Maybe his final plan was coming together.

Stam Chaguartay allowed himself a rare smile.

'That's a lot of fruit,' Clar exclaimed, squinting at the man's name badge. 'Ahji.'

'Would you like me to take some away?' asked Ahji, without enthusiasm.

Clar had a sense that he would rather be somewhere else, possibly because that place had somewhere to sit. Ahji did not look like a man who got a lot of satisfaction from his job. He looked like a man who would appreciate a sit down.

'What? No, I…' Clar looked again at the table at the far end of the conference room, laden with exotic fruit of pretty much every colour. 'Other people might want some. This isn't all for me. Is it?'

'If you want it to be.' Ahji's smile was pleasant enough. 'Or if you prefer, I can remove it. Would you like pastries instead? Or if you're not hungry, a floral display, maybe.'

'It's fine.' Clar felt guilty about all the fuss. 'Leave it there.'

'If there is anything else, anything at all I can do, please do not hesitate to call,' continued Ahji. 'My name is, of course, Ahji, and you can contact me via the button that has been added to the home screen of your Com device for the duration of your time at Administration.'

With that, Ahji strolled out, leaving Clar alone in the vast meeting room. They looked around. Apart from the massive pile of fruit, there was already a floral display, so they weren't sure why they would need another.

There was also an area to dispense hot drinks, a cocktail cabinet that it was too early for, however weird today was already getting and, on the closest table, a small selection of cosmetics, with a pile of what looked to be the fluffiest looking face towels Clar had ever seen.

They picked one up. It was, indeed, breathtakingly fluffy. In one corner, in deep blue, were embroidered the initials CT.

No. That stands for something else. They haven't monogrammed towels just for my visit…

Clar had assumed, when they'd initially been ushered in, that this was some sort of green room for journalists waiting to interview the Mayor. That was the audience that they had been granted, and they hadn't presumed that their access was exclusive.

Increasingly, they thought it was. An exclusive interview in an exclusive meeting room with Mayor Chaguartay. This all seemed way over the top, especially for a foreign journalist broadcasting on a niche channel.

Clar was suspicious. They'd set this whole thing up to test the water, see what Chaguartay knew, see if they could sniff out any involvement in Sim's investigation, and therefore in Sim's disappearance.

The special treatment they were getting unsettled them. How close to the truth were they getting? How dangerous was that?

They wandered across the vast room and picked up what they assumed to be an apple. It looked apple-like, although it was a brighter red than they had ever seen, and had a deeper shine than seemed entirely natural.

They turned it over a few times in their hand. This was wrong. Every instinct they had was telling them they needed to get out.

Screw the access. Screw the exclusive access.

Dear Creator, that sentence hurt to think.

But they felt like they were about to lose something. Either their journalistic integrity or their life. They weren't sure they were quite ready to give up on either.

Clar put the apple down and turned to collect their bag. A man was standing in the doorway.

They'd expected Mayor Chaguartay himself, a man who, in their head, was slimy and grotesque, an obese cesspool of a human being, greasy with the spittle of a thousand lies, smeared in the blood of a thousand downtrodden workers.

This man was not that. He was tall and well built and, whilst not athletic, not unfit. He was flattered by the expensive suit and his hair was slicked back. Or still wet?

This must be Manukan's replacement. But he looked like the Mayor. Younger, more attractive, but with a definite resemblance. Chaguartay had no male relatives that Clar knew of. Two daughters, no grandchildren. This was also confusing.

'Excuse me, Mx Triebel, for sneaking up on you like that,' he spoke softly, and had obviously noticed Clar startle when they saw him, 'and for coming straight from the gym.'

He indicated his wet hair.

'The facilities here are excellent. Feel free to avail yourself of them after your conversation.'

Clar swallowed hard. They weren't leaving, then.

'Mr...?' they asked.

'Chaguartay,' said the man.

A relative, after all. Must have come from out of town.

'Related?' They blurted it out.

It felt disempowering, this loss of control, loss of the calm and collected air that they usually projected. Clar's skin crawled slightly at the thought, but they had to admit that they were attracted to this man.

'Nephew. The Mayor thought he would feel more comfortable if his closest aides were people he could trust implicitly.'

Clar noted that. A lack of trust. They wondered whether that was a reference to Manukan. Clar had heard the rumours. There weren't any follow-up questions they felt safe to ask.

Best move on.

'Well, I'm all ready when the Mayor is.'

Clar indicated a chair and moved to draw one up herself. Chaguartay's nephew didn't move from the doorway.

'Ah, you're keen to get started. That is excellent. I am pleased to see that. However, this room is a little... public for my uncle..'

Is it? thought Clar. They were just thinking that it wasn't public enough.

'Come with me,' he said, turning and starting down the plushly furnished corridor. 'He keeps a private office here. You will be more comfortable there.'

'Of course he does, of course we will,' mouthed Clar, eyebrows raised at the man's retreating back.

They should bail now. If there was one thing they were certain of in the moment, it was that they should not, under any circumstances, get into the lift that was so conveniently opening as this new Chaguartay approached it.

I'll probably never come out again.

It made sense for Chaguartay to have his own facilities. Apart from his importance, his daughter worked here, in Administration. If the rumours were to be believed, father and daughter hadn't spoken in years. She was married to the

Opposition candidate for the mayoralty. That would be an awkward encounter.

Clar pulled themselves together. This was a chance to interview the most powerful man in Trinity, to pose tough questions, maybe even get some answers.

There was something strange going on here, the red carpet treatment, the prodigal nephew, Manukan, Sim. Clar could smell a story. They were certain that Sim was onto something. Now they were onto it too. They just had to figure it out before it got them killed.

Besides, who were they if not someone who would, without a second thought, abandon all concern for their own personal safety, when a puzzle was presented, when a story was begging to be told?

They were Clar Triebel, and Clar Triebel didn't run away.

Clar picked up their bag and strode after Mayor Chaguartay's aide. By the time the lift doors slid closed and they caught their reflection in the gold wall in front of them, they had that look in their eye.

They weren't leaving until they had their story.

THE BEGINNING

Welcome to the Entanglement series!

Book 1: Echoes

Who can you trust if you can't trust yourself?

Estrel Beck doesn't want to be a software salesman. Yet here he is, newly arrived in the city-state of Trinity, for a make-or-break meeting with the local Administration department. Under-prepared, under-motivated and over-sensitive, every little thing about this strange place seems to stress Estrel out. When he discovers a message scrawled on the back of a napkin, in his own handwriting, telling him he's trapped in a time loop, he knows for sure that he's in over his head. Then the Administration building explodes.

As Estrel struggles to make sense of his situation and find an escape, he is drawn into Trinity's bizarre underworld and the struggles for power against Trinity's corrupt Mayor Chaguartay. Science fiction meets urban thriller - Echoes is a story about being trapped by your past choices and what it takes to break free.

Book 2: Entrapment

Before you can save the future, you have to fix the past.

Once upon a time, Estrel Beck arrived in Trinity for the first time.. THREE WEEKS EARLIER:

Simeon Lagrange is an Oficier in service to Trinity Authority. He's got a lot on his plate - including a monk who shouldn't exist, an outsider carrying a mysterious package and an ex-lover seeking justice.

Ordered to investigate the shooting of Ralph Manukan, an aide to the unpopular Mayor Chaguartay, Lagrange reluctantly accepts the assignment. But every lead unravels, revealing a city steeped in dysfunction that conspires against him.

Soon, Lagrange's own inner demons, and the weight of his past mistakes, threaten to overshadow his quest for the truth. In the city where past and future collide, every step towards unravelling the present exposes secrets that could reshape destiny.

It looks like you've finished reading WELCOME TO TRINITY...

Thank you!

I really hope you enjoyed it, and if you did it would be great if you could pass the message on! Post on social media about this great book you read... maybe even tell a friend in real life... whatever you can do to spread the word would be fantastic and make all the difference for me, struggling little indie author that I am.

Next, if you'd like to stay up to date with what I'm writing and when you can read it, pop along to philoddy.com where you can find links to my own socials. There's also a link for your friends to sign up for my newsletter and get their own copy of Welcome To Trinity.

Finally, there are other books I've written and contributed to. You should definitely buy all of these, right now...

ENTANGLEMENT SERIES
Echoes
Entrapment
Eclipse (coming early 2025)
Enlightenment (coming late 2025)
Exodus (coming 2026)

FOR CHILDREN
The Man In The Moon

AS CONTRIBUTOR

Royston and District Writers' Circle 40th Anniversary Anthology

There Are Many Ways Of Getting Lost: The Royston Writers' Circle Lockdown Anthology

About the Author

Phil Oddy lives in North Hertfordshire and writes stories about how to cope in a confusing world, cleverly disguised as sci-fi/fantasy adventures. Find his website at https://philoddy.com - everything he's currently up to should be on there.

He is happily married with two sons, and has promised everyone lavish gifts if he ever writes a bestseller, so if you've bought one of his books then they all thank you.

Despite a long and successful career as an IT analyst in both the public and private sectors, writing is something he seems to be unable to prevent himself doing which means that by encouraging him you're either feeding an addiction or providing therapy. You can pick which.

When his fingers are too tired to carry on typing, Phil likes to relax by reading something by David Mitchell (either one is fine) or binge-watching Drag Race.

Printed in Great Britain
by Amazon